This igloo book belongs to:

....

igloobooks

Published in 2019
by Igloo Books Ltd
Cottage Farm
Sywell
NN6 0BJ
www.igloobooks.com

Copyright © 2014 Igloo Books Ltd
Igloo Books is an imprint of Bonnier Books UK

1119 001
2 4 6 8 10 9 7 5 3 1
ISBN 978-1-78905-684-6

Illustrated by Cee Biscoe

Printed and manufactured in China

The Happy
Postbunny

igloobooks

It was Bunny's birthday and she couldn't wait to pick some
juicy carrots as a special treat. Outside, she spotted Postman Owl
in the sky and some envelopes scattered on the ground,
all addressed to Bunny's friends.

"You've dropped your letters!" called Bunny, but Owl didn't hear.
Then, Bunny had a wonderful idea. "I'll deliver the letters myself,"
she thought. "It will be so much fun to be a postbunny for a day."
So Bunny hopped on her way to Mouse's house first.

When Mouse found his letter outside Mouse Hole, he tore it open eagerly.
It was an invitation from Owl to a surprise party for Bunny!
"You are the best-dressed animal in Blossom Forest," read Mouse.
"Please come to the party in your most special clothes!"

Mouse felt very flattered indeed. He flung open his wardrobe doors and searched through every drawer. "How will I ever find the perfect outfit in time for the party?" he wondered, looking for his special bow tie.

Squirrel received her invitation next and
she read the letter out loud, full of excitement.
"You're the best baker in all of Blossom Forest," she read.
"Please can you make one of your famous
birthday cakes for Bunny's party?"

Squirrel beamed with pride and set to work straight away. "Bunny is sure to love this delicious carrot icing," she said, mixing the ingredients in her best mixing bowl.

Before long, Bunny had hopped
all the way through Toadstool Hollow
and arrived at Hedgehog's house.
"What brings you to this side of
the forest?" asked Hedgehog.

To Hedgehog
Willow Tree Log
Blossom Forest

To Badger
Bramble Brook

"Owl dropped his letters outside
my burrow," explained Bunny.
"This one is for you!"
"How kind of you to deliver it,"
said Hedgehog, scampering inside.

To Hedgehog
Willow Tree Log
Blossom Forest

1st

Hedgehog's invitation from Owl asked him
to bring some presents to the party, as he was so good
at wrapping gifts. "I have just the thing!" cried Hedgehog,
as he gathered his pretty paper and special ribbon.

Bunny was beginning to feel warm in the sunshine, so she went to dip her paws in Bramble Brook. "Badger's house is just across the water," thought Bunny, so she hopped over Pebble Bridge to deliver his letter.

To Badger
Bramble Brook Sett
Blossom Forest

Bunny hopped on her way, as Badger peered
at the envelope and read the invitation slowly.

"Your house is always decorated so beautifully," he read.
"Please bring some of your lovely decorations to the party."

Badger thought for a moment and smiled.
"I'll bring the best balloons anyone has ever seen!" he said,
blowing up so many bright and shiny balloons that they
filled the whole room. "Phew!" puffed Badger.

Soon, Bunny had delivered every single one
of the letters. She hopped all the way through
Sunflower Meadow and back to her burrow.
There, she spotted a letter she
hadn't noticed earlier.

"It's a birthday card for me!" cried Bunny.
Inside the card, it said there was a surprise
at the Old Enchanted Oak Tree that evening.
"I wonder who sent it?" thought Bunny, as she
hopped inside to pick out her outfit.

Bunny

When Bunny arrived at the Old Enchanted Oak Tree, she couldn't believe her eyes. There were piles of presents and a table of delicious food. All her friends were gathered around, wearing party hats. "Surprise!" they shouted. Bunny giggled. "Did I deliver the invitations for my own surprise party?" she asked.

Postman Owl, perched on the branch above her, gave a hoot and nodded. "I dropped the invitations by mistake," he said, "but I knew you would deliver them. You're the kindest bunny in Blossom Forest."

Bunny took a bite of her cake. "This is the best surprise, ever!" she said.

The next day, Bunny was really grateful to her friends for planning such a wonderful surprise. She decided to write a very special note to them all. "This will be the perfect thank you letter," she said, reading it aloud.

Just to say...

Thank you

To my wonderful friends,

Thank you so much for my fantastic birthday party. It was an amazing surprise!

Squirrel's cake was delicious, Mouse looked wonderful in his bow tie and the Old Enchanted Oak Tree looked magical with Badger's decorations. The gifts Hedgehog wrapped all looked so pretty, too.

I must say a special thank you to Postman Owl for planning the surprise. I would love to be the postbunny for one more day if you would ever like a day off!

Lots of love,

Bunny
xxx